Dorothy Corey
Illustrations by Nancy Poydar

Will There Be a Lap for Me?

ALBERT WHITMAN & COMPANY, Morton Grove, Illinois

Library of Congress Cataloging-in-Publication Data

Corey, Dorothy.
   Will there be a lap for me? / Dorothy Corey;
illustrations by Nancy Poydar.
        p.   cm.
   Summary: Kyle misses his time on Mother's lap while
she is pregnant and is happy when the birth of his baby
brother makes her lap available again.
   ISBN 0-8075-9109-2 (hardcover)
   ISBN 0-8075-9110-6 (paperback)
   [1. Mothers and sons—Fiction.   2. Babies—Fiction.]
I. Poydar, Nancy, ill.   II. Title.
PZ7.C815395WI   1992   91-20324
[E]—dc20   CIP
                                                   AC

The text for this book is set in Benguiat.
The illustrations are in watercolor and colored pencil.
The book design is by Susan B. Cohn.

For Joanna Corey, with love from Nana. *D.C.*

For my husband, Hank, and our two sons,
Henry and Eric. *N.P.*

Kyle had a special place.
It was not too hard
and not too soft.
It was just right for resting
and talking
and listening to stories
and watching the birds.

But Mother's stomach grew larger
and larger
and larger
until it was very large indeed.

And Kyle's special place became smaller
and smaller
and smaller
until it had almost completely disappeared.
A new baby was growing inside Mother!
Soon the baby would be born.

Mother put her arm around Kyle. "Rest beside me," she said.

Kyle snuggled against Mother. He slid his hands across her great big stomach. Enormous!

Would he be able to feel their baby moving around tonight?

Sure enough, he could! That little rascal was really kicking up a storm!

"Look!" Kyle shouted. "See this lump! He's poking his fist up at me!"

This was all quite wonderful to Kyle. But snuggling beside Mother was not the same as sitting on her lap.

Daddy's lap
    was too hard and bumpy.

(The babysitter
    hardly had a lap at all!)

Grandma's lap
    was too soft and squishy.

The hours went by.
The days went by.
The weeks went by.
And Kyle still missed his special place.

One day he waited and waited with Grandma . . .

Then Kyle had a new baby brother, a baby
brother named Matt!
   Kyle was *very* excited!

But he still missed his special place. Mother
was so busy. Baby Matt *always* needed something.

Kyle was grumpy. Mother was feeding
Baby Matt AGAIN!

"Sit with us, Pickle Puss," Mother begged.
"We both want you very much!"

"You do?" asked Kyle.

"OF COURSE WE DO!" said Mother.

Kyle cuddled close to Mother and
Baby Matt on the couch. With his fingertips,
he stroked the baby's smooth, silky skin.

Up and down,
up and down,
gently,
gently.

Yet, Kyle felt a little sad. That Baby Matt
was hungry ALL THE TIME! And Kyle still
missed his special place.

In the afternoon while Baby Matt was sleeping, Mother called to Kyle.

"Our new bird feeder came today, Hon. Isn't it pretty? Let's put some seed in it. We can watch the birds together,
    just Kyle and Mother,
    just Mother and Kyle."

Kyle climbed up on Mother's lap once more.
It was not too hard
and not too soft.
It was just right for resting
and talking
and listening to stories

and watching the birds.